BAD DO

Meet Gus, Ken, Ben, and Jen—
four normal kids . . .
I am hungry.
Want some gum?
ZIP
. . . or are they?
What was that?
MEEEEOW!

Hey! My paper!
NEWS
My flowers!
Yo, guys—I think Spike is loose.
MEOW
Help! My cat!
GRRR!

This looks like a job for . . .
We have to stop him!
Gum Bo
Yes!
Wedgie Boy
You bet!
Yo-Yo Girl
Do we *have* to?
The Whiner

. . . the Fearless Four!
Ready!
Ready!
Ready!
You guys! I am still hungry.
Yo! Spike! Over here!
Yo! Guys! A little help, please!
GRRR!

They distract the dog . . .
Watch this, Spike.
STRETCH!
mail
Look this way!
ZOING!
Over here!
Look at me!
ZIP!

. . . so Gum Bo can work.
Okay, bubble gum—let us show her what you can do!
SMACK!
THWACK!
Here. Let me help you.
Why, thank you!

But the danger is not over.
Yo! What do we do now?
Do not look at me!
GRRR!
Guys! I am really, really, REALLY hungry!!!
YIKE!

He is running away!
ZOOM!
Hooray!
Look at him go!
Yo! Nice job, Whiner!
Now can we eat?

Play Ball

Another day, another whine.
ZIP
CHEW
I am bored.
Want to try my yo-yo?
No.
Hey! We can play ball!

Can we play?
Sorry.
No ball.
No ball?
Where is it?
Over there.

All mine!
Ball Hog
All over town, kids have been robbed!
This looks like another job for—
—the Fearless Four!
Not again!

Yo! Give back those balls!
Please.

Make me!
Do not worry. I have a plan.
What do we do now?
Hog

Gum Bo adds gum to his ball.
Well, look at this! I have a ball!
Give me that!
You bet.

My hands!
THWUCK!
THWAP!
THWOMP!
THWICK!
My feet!
WHIMPER
I think I will tie up these loose ends!

Are you *done* yet?
Yep.
SNIFFLE

Hey, guys! Come get your balls!
Ball

YAY!
YIPPEE!!
Ball Hog

At last, everyone was happy . . .
Ouch!
BOINK!
Home run!
Yay!

. . . well, almost everyone.
WAAAHHH!

Stop That Sock!

ICE
Where is the ice cream man?
Look!
Check it out!

Just one bad guy could have done this—The Sock!
No one can stop The Sock!
He wants to take over the town!
TOWN HALL
We have to stop him!
Do we have to?

The Sock is so smelly!
You are so right!
Gum Bo has the right super tool for the job!
Here!
Now we are ready!
Let us go!
Ouch! This thing hurts.

HOT DOG
Yo! There he is!
What do we do now?
I am thirsty!
That is it!
Hey, guys. I have a plan.
WHISPER
WHISPER

Moments later:
THWACK!
SWOOSH!
SOAP
ZWUP!

What a blast!
ACK!

Yo! We did it!
We washed The Sock!
I got soap in my eye!

This is not the last you will smell of me!
I will be back!
SQUISH
SQUISH

We will be ready!
Guys! My eye!